This Prayer Journal Belongs To

Published by RKSPUBLISHING

Thank You

James 1:19

My dear brothers and sisters, take note of this. (Everyone should be)

Quick to litsen, slow to speak and slow to become angey.

•••

2 Timothy 1:7

"For God did not give us a spirit of timidity, but a spirit of power, of love and self-discipline."

... God wants you to know Him

Todays's verse...

Date

Lord teach me...

Lord guide me...

Today I pray for...

Prayers for others...

Answered prayers...

Todays's verse...

Date

Lord teach me...

Lord guide me...

Today I pray for...

Prayers for others...

Answered prayers...

Todays's verse...

Date

Lord teach me...

Lord guide me...

Today I pray for...

Prayers for others...

Answered prayers...

Todays's verse...

Date

Lord teach me...

Lord guide me...

Today I pray for...

Prayers for others...

Answered prayers...

Todays's verse...

Date

Lord teach me...

Lord guide me...

Today I pray for...

Prayers for others...

Answered prayers...

Todays's verse...

Date

Lord teach me...

Lord guide me...

Today I pray for...

Prayers for others...

Answered prayers...

Todays's verse...

Date

Lord teach me...

Lord guide me...

Today I pray for...

Prayers for others...

Answered prayers...

Todays's verse...

Date

Lord teach me...

Lord guide me...

Today I pray for...

Prayers for others...

Answered prayers...

Todays's verse...

Date

Lord teach me...

Lord guide me...

Today I pray for...

Prayers for others...

Answered prayers...

Todays's verse...

Date

Lord teach me...

Lord guide me...

Today I pray for...

Prayers for others...

Answered prayers...

Todays's verse...

Date

Lord teach me...

Lord guide me...

Today I pray for...

Prayers for others...

Answered prayers...

Todays's verse...

Date

Lord teach me...

Lord guide me...

Today I pray for...

Prayers for others...

Answered prayers...

Todays's verse...

Date

Lord teach me...

Lord guide me...

Today I pray for...

Prayers for others...

Answered prayers...

Todays's verse...

Date

Lord teach me...

Lord guide me...

Today I pray for...

Prayers for others...

Answered prayers...

Todays's verse...

Date

Lord
teach me...

Lord guide me...

Today I pray for...

Prayers for others...

Answered prayers...

Todays's verse...

Date

Lord
teach me...

Lord guide me...

Today I pray for...

Prayers for others...

Answered prayers...

Todays's verse...

Date

Lord
teach me...

Lord guide me...

Today I pray for...

Prayers for others...

Answered prayers...

Todays's verse...

Date

Lord teach me...

Lord guide me...

Today I pray for...

Prayers for others...

Answered prayers...

Todays's verse...

Date

Lord teach me...

Lord guide me...

Today I pray for...

Prayers for others...

Answered prayers...

Todays's verse...

Date

Lord
teach me...

Lord guide me...

Today I pray for...

Prayers for others...

Answered prayers...

Todays's verse...

Date

Lord teach me...

Lord guide me...

Today I pray for...

Prayers for others...

Answered prayers...

Todays's verse... Date

Lord teach me...

Lord guide me...

Today I pray for...

Prayers for others...

Answered prayers...

Todays's verse...

Date

Lord teach me...

Lord guide me...

Today I pray for...

Prayers for others...

Answered prayers...

Todays's verse...

Date

Lord teach me...

Lord guide me...

Today I pray for...

Prayers for others...

Answered prayers...

Todays's verse...

Date

Lord teach me...

Lord guide me...

Today I pray for...

Prayers for others...

Answered prayers...

Todays's verse... Date

Lord teach me...

Lord guide me...

Today I pray for...

Prayers for others...

Answered prayers...

Todays's verse...

Date

Lord teach me...

Lord guide me...

Today I pray for...

Prayers for others...

Answered prayers...

Todays's verse... Date

Lord teach me...

Lord guide me...

Today I pray for...

Prayers for others...

Answered prayers...

Todays's verse... Date

Lord teach me...

Lord guide me...

Today I pray for...

Prayers for others...

Answered prayers...

Todays's verse...

Date

Lord
teach me...

Lord guide me...

Today I pray for...

Prayers for others...

Answered prayers...

Todays's verse...

Date

Lord teach me...

Lord guide me...

Today I pray for...

Prayers for others...

Answered prayers...

Todays's verse...

Date

Lord teach me...

Lord guide me...

Today I pray for...

Prayers for others...

Answered prayers...

Todays's verse...

Date

Lord teach me...

Lord guide me...

Today I pray for...

Prayers for others...

Answered prayers...

Today's's verse...

Date

Lord teach me...

Lord guide me...

Today I pray for...

Prayers for others...

Answered prayers...

Todays's verse... Date

Lord
teach me...

Lord guide me...

Today I pray for...

Prayers for others...

Answered prayers...

Todays's verse...

Date

Lord teach me...

Lord guide me...

Today I pray for...

Prayers for others...

Answered prayers...

Todays's verse... Date

Lord
teach me...

Lord guide me...

Today I pray for...

Prayers for others...

Answered prayers...

Todays's verse...

Date

Lord
teach me...

Lord guide me...

Today I pray for...

Prayers for others...

Answered prayers...

Todays's verse... Date

Lord teach me...

Lord guide me...

Today I pray for...

Prayers for others...

Answered prayers...

Todays's verse...

Date

Lord teach me...

Lord guide me...

Today I pray for...

Prayers for others...

Answered prayers...

Todays's verse... Date

Lord teach me...

Lord guide me...

Today I pray for...

Prayers for others...

Answered prayers...

Todays's verse...

Date

Lord teach me...

Lord guide me...

Today I pray for...

Prayers for others...

Answered prayers...

Todays's verse...

Date

Lord
teach me...

Lord guide me...

Today I pray for...

Prayers for others...

Answered prayers...

Todays's verse...

Date

Lord teach me...

Lord guide me...

Today I pray for...

Prayers for others...

Answered prayers...

Todays's verse...

Date

Lord teach me...

Lord guide me...

Today I pray for...

Prayers for others...

Answered prayers...

Todays's verse...

Date

Lord
teach me...

Lord guide me...

Today I pray for...

Prayers for others...

Answered prayers...

Todays's verse...

Date

Lord teach me...

Lord guide me...

Today I pray for...

Prayers for others...

Answered prayers...

Todays's verse...

Date

Lord teach me...

Lord guide me...

Today I pray for...

Prayers for others...

Answered prayers...

Todays's verse...

Date

Lord teach me...

Lord guide me...

Today I pray for...

Prayers for others...

Answered prayers...

Todays's verse...

Date

Lord teach me...

Lord guide me...

Today I pray for...

Prayers for others...

Answered prayers...

Todays's verse...

Date

Lord teach me...

Lord guide me...

Today I pray for...

Prayers for others...

Answered prayers...

Todays's verse...

Date

Lord teach me...

Lord guide me...

Today I pray for...

Prayers for others...

Answered prayers...

Todays's verse...

Date

Lord teach me...

Lord guide me...

Today I pray for...

Prayers for others...

Answered prayers...

Todays's verse...

Date

Lord teach me...

Lord guide me...

Today I pray for...

Prayers for others...

Answered prayers...

Todays's verse...

Date

Lord teach me...

Lord guide me...

Today I pray for...

Prayers for others...

Answered prayers...

Todays's verse...

Date

Lord teach me...

Lord guide me...

Today I pray for...

Prayers for others...

Answered prayers...

Todays's verse...

Date

Lord teach me...

Lord guide me...

Today I pray for...

Prayers for others...

Answered prayers...

Todays's verse... Date

Lord
teach me...

Lord guide me...

Today I pray for...

Prayers for others...

Answered prayers...

Todays's verse...

Date

Lord teach me...

Lord guide me...

Today I pray for...

Prayers for others...

Answered prayers...

Todays's verse...

Date

Lord teach me...

Lord guide me...

Today I pray for...

Prayers for others...

Answered prayers...

Todays's verse...   Date

Lord
teach me...

Lord guide me...

Today I pray for...

Prayers for others...

Answered prayers...

Todays's verse...

Date

Lord teach me...

Lord guide me...

Today I pray for...

Prayers for others...

Answered prayers...

Todays's verse...

Date

Lord teach me...

Lord guide me...

Today I pray for...

Prayers for others...

Answered prayers...

Todays's verse...

Date

Lord teach me...

Lord guide me...

Today I pray for...

Prayers for others...

Answered prayers...

Todays's verse...

Date

Lord teach me...

Lord guide me...

Today I pray for...

Prayers for others...

Answered prayers...

Todays's verse...

Date

Lord teach me...

Lord guide me...

Today I pray for...

Prayers for others...

Answered prayers...

Todays's verse... Date

Lord
teach me...

Lord guide me...

Today I pray for...

Prayers for others...

Answered prayers...

Todays's verse...

Date

Lord teach me...

Lord guide me...

Today I pray for...

Prayers for others...

Answered prayers...

Todays's verse...

Date

Lord
teach me...

Lord guide me...

Today I pray for...

Prayers for others...

Answered prayers...

Todays's verse...

Date

Lord teach me...

Lord guide me...

Today I pray for...

Prayers for others...

Answered prayers...

Todays's verse...

Date

Lord
teach me...

Lord guide me...

Today I pray for...

Prayers for others...

Answered prayers...

Todays's verse...

Date

Lord teach me...

Lord guide me...

Today I pray for...

Prayers for others...

Answered prayers...

Todays's verse...

Date

Lord teach me...

Lord guide me...

Today I pray for...

Prayers for others...

Answered prayers...

Todays's verse...

Date

Lord teach me...

Lord guide me...

Today I pray for...

Prayers for others...

Answered prayers...

Todays's verse...

Date

Lord teach me...

Lord guide me...

Today I pray for...

Prayers for others...

Answered prayers...

Todays's verse...

Date

Lord teach me...

Lord guide me...

Today I pray for...

Prayers for others...

Answered prayers...

Todays's verse...

Date

Lord
teach me...

Lord guide me...

Today I pray for...

Prayers for others...

Answered prayers...

Todays's verse...

Date

Lord
teach me...

Lord guide me...

Today I pray for...

Prayers for others...

Answered prayers...

Todays's verse...

Date

Lord teach me...

Lord guide me...

Today I pray for...

Prayers for others...

Answered prayers...

Todays's verse...

Date

Lord teach me...

Lord guide me...

Today I pray for...

Prayers for others...

Answered prayers...

Todays's verse...   Date

Lord
teach me...

Lord guide me...

Today I pray for...

Prayers for others...

Answered prayers...

Todays's verse...

Date

Lord teach me...

Lord guide me...

Today I pray for...

Prayers for others...

Answered prayers...

Todays's verse...

Date

Lord
teach me...

Lord guide me...

Today I pray for...

Prayers for others...

Answered prayers...

Todays's verse...

Date

Lord
teach me...

Lord guide me...

Today I pray for...

Prayers for others...

Answered prayers...

Todays's verse...

Date

Lord
teach me...

Lord guide me...

Today I pray for...

Prayers for others...

Answered prayers...

Todays's verse...

Date

Lord teach me...

Lord guide me...

Today I pray for...

Prayers for others...

Answered prayers...

Todays's verse...

Date

Lord teach me...

Lord guide me...

Today I pray for...

Prayers for others...

Answered prayers...

Todays's verse...

Date

Lord teach me...

Lord guide me...

Today I pray for...

Prayers for others...

Answered prayers...

Todays's verse...

Date

Lord teach me...

Lord guide me...

Today I pray for...

Prayers for others...

Answered prayers...

Todays's verse...

Date

Lord
teach me...

Lord guide me...

Today I pray for...

Prayers for others...

Answered prayers...

Made in the USA
Las Vegas, NV
25 January 2024

84875983R00103